Mrs Simkin and the Magic Wheelbarrow
Linda Allen

Illustrated by
Margaret Chamberlain

Hamish Hamilton
London

HAMISH HAMILTON CHILDREN'S BOOKS

Published by the Penguin Group
27 Wrights Lane, London W8 5TZ, England
Viking Penguin Inc, 40 West 23rd Street, New York, New York 10010, U.S.A.
Penguin Books Australia Ltd, Ringwood, Victoria, Australia
Penguin Books Canada Ltd, 2801 John Street, Markham, Ontario, Canada L3R 1B4
Penguin Books (N.Z.) Ltd, 182-190 Wairau Road, Auckland 10, New Zealand

Penguin Books Ltd, Registered Offices: Harmondsworth, Middlesex, England

First published in Great Britain 1987 by
Hamish Hamilton Children's Books

Text copyright © 1987 by Linda Allen
Illustrations copyright © 1987 by Margaret Chamberlain

3 5 7 9 10 8 6 4

British Library Cataloguing in Publication Data
CIP data for this book is available from the British Library

ISBN 0–241–11992–8

Typeset by Katerprint Typesetting Services, Oxford
Printed in Hong Kong by
Imago Publishing

One day Mrs Simkin bought a new wheelbarrow. It was bright yellow with a red wheel and green handles.

Mr Simkin said it was much too pretty to use for carrying the garden rubbish.

"But what else can we use it for?" said
Mrs Simkin. She thought for a moment.
"I know!" she cried. "We can use it for
riding in."

"Good idea!" said Mr Simkin. "Jump in and I will give you a ride."

So Mrs Simkin jumped into the wheelbarrow and Mr Simkin pushed her around the garden. Then they swapped places. It was great fun.

The lady next door looked over the
hedge to see what was happening.

"Why are you sitting in that
wheelbarrow?" she asked.

Mrs Simkin told her that she was
having a ride.

The lady next door said it was a very
silly thing to do.

But Mrs Simkin laughed. "But it's a
magic wheelbarrow," she said. "The only
magic wheelbarrow in the world. When I
sit in it I don't feel like Mrs Simkin any
more. I feel like a queen."

"Magic wheelbarrow indeed! What
nonsense!" said the lady next door. And
she went away, looking cross.

All day long the wheelbarrow stood in the garden, just like any other wheelbarrow.

Mrs Simkin put pots of flowers in it and Mr Simkin tied ribbons around the handles. It looked very smart.

When it was bedtime Mrs Simkin said, "Let's go outside and say goodnight to the wheelbarrow before we go to bed."

"Good idea," said Mr Simkin.

"It's a beautiful night," said Mr
Simkin. "Would you like a ride?"

"Oh yes!" cried Mrs Simkin. "That
would be lovely."

She got into the wheelbarrow, and as
soon as she sat down something wonderful
happened.

Suddenly Mrs Simkin was sitting in a beautiful boat. Mr Simkin was standing at the back, dressed in a black and silver cloak. On his head he had a large blue hat. He had grown curly whiskers.

Mr Simkin pushed the boat along with
a pole and began to sing. Mrs Simkin
joined in. She was very happy. They
sailed around the garden in the
moonlight.

After a while the boat became a
wheelbarrow again. Mr and Mrs Simkin
went indoors and had some cocoa.

"It really *is* a magic wheelbarrow,"
said Mrs Simkin as they went upstairs to
bed.

The next morning, Mr Robinson, the milkman came by.

"A little bird tells me that you have a magic wheelbarrow," he said.

"Quite true," replied Mr Simkin. "Come and look."

Mr Robinson said it was a very nice wheelbarrow, but he did not believe that it was a magic one.

Mr Simkin gave him a ride, but nothing magical happened.

"Try sitting backwards," said Mrs
Simkin.
But that didn't work, either.

"I cannot understand it," said Mrs Simkin. "It's a magic wheelbarrow when I sit in it."

"Perhaps you are the one who makes the magic, my dear," said Mr Simkin. "If you sit in the wheelbarrow with Mr Robinson it is sure to work."

But still nothing magical happened.
The lady next door said she had never
seen such a thing in her life.

When night-time came again, Mrs Simkin climbed into the wheelbarrow all by herself.

Suddenly she was sitting upon a magnificent white horse. Mr Simkin was sitting behind her. They galloped round and round the garden.

The lady next door was watching
them. And she couldn't believe her eyes!

When morning came, she told all the
people in the street what she had seen.

Nobody believed her.

"Then come to my house tonight," she
said, "and see what happens."

That night the moon was very bright.
It was almost as light as day.

Mrs Simkin said, "Our wheelbarrow is
sure to turn into something very special
tonight, Stanley."

Mr and Mrs Simkin didn't know that all the people were watching over the hedge.

As Mrs Simkin stepped into the wheelbarrow . . .

23

it turned into a magnificent glass coach.

Mrs Simkin had a crown on her head. Mr Simkin had a top hat.

The coach was drawn by six white horses.

The lady next door tried to keep the people quiet, but they were too excited. When Mrs Simkin passed by in her coach they all cheered.

Mrs Simkin bowed to them, and waved like a queen.

The next day all the people who lived in the street went to buy new wheelbarrows.

They waited until it was night-time and then they gave each other rides. Everyone had a lot of fun, but nothing magical happened. The wheelbarrows weren't magic ones, like Mrs Simkin's.

The people were disappointed. They
went to Mrs Simkin's house to complain.

"We have all bought wheelbarrows,"
they said. "They look just like yours, but
they won't change into anything special.
We have spent our money for nothing."

"We told the lady next door that our wheelbarrow was the only magic wheelbarrow in the world," said Mr Simkin. "You can't blame us."

But the people were so cross that Mrs Simkin said, "Listen. I will buy your wheelbarrows if you don't want them any more. I like to have plenty of wheelbarrows about the place."

She gave the people their money and they left their wheelbarrows in her garden.

That night Mrs Simkin said, "Come out into the garden, Stanley. I want you to do something for me." And she told Mr Simkin to tie the wheelbarrows together, all in a row.

When the moon was high in the sky, Mrs Simkin stepped into the first wheelbarrow.

And then something truly magical happened . . .

"All aboard!" cried Mr Simkin, waving his flag.